MATT CHRISTOPHER®

#2
DAY OF THE DRAGON

Text by Stephanie Peters
Illustrated by Michael Koelsch

LITTLE, BROWN AND COMPANY

New York ~ Boston

Little, Brown and Company

Time Warner Book Group
1271 Avenue of the Americas, New York, NY 10020
Visit our Web site at www.lb-kids.com

First Edition

The characters and events portrayed in this book are fictitious.
Any similarity to real persons, living or dead, is coincidental
and not intended by the author.

Matt Christopher® is a registered trademark
of Catherine M. Christopher.

Library of Congress Cataloging-in-Publication Data
Christopher, Matt.
Day of the dragon / text by Stephanie Peters ;
illustrated by Michael Koelsch — 1st ed.
p.   cm. — (The extreme team ; #2)
Summary: While studying kung fu to try to overcome
his clumsiness, Mark learns something that may interfere
with his friends' plans for a group Halloween costume.
ISBN 0-316-73751-8 (hc) / ISBN 0-316-73753-4 (pb)
[1. Kung fu — Fiction.   2. Friendship — Fiction.
3. Halloween — Fiction.   4. Costume — Fiction.]
I. Koelsch, Michael, ill.   II. Title.   III. Series.
PZ7.P441833Da 2004   2003054554
                [Fic] — dc22

HC: 10   9   8   7   6   5   4   3   2   1
PB: 10   9   8   7   6   5   4   3   2   1

WOR (hc)

COM-MO (pb)

Printed in the United States of America

CHAPTER ONE

Mark Goldstein took off his glasses, wiped them clean, and put them back on again. *I'll never be able to do this,* he thought. Alison Lee, the teenager who kept watch over the town skatepark, was demonstrating a skateboard move called the kickflip. Mark and his friends, Savannah Smith and Belicia "Bizz" Juarez, were about to try it for the first time.

"You guys can do ollies, right?" Alison asked. Mark and the girls nodded. "Well, the kickflip is like an ollie. Except when the board is in the air, it flips around, like a barrel rolling. Here, let me show you."

She put her left foot on the board's kicktail. Her

right foot went between the front and back trucks. "With an ollie, your front foot is sideways. With the kickflip, it's at an angle." She turned her right foot. "Think of the board as a clock face. The nose is at twelve o'clock. Point your foot between ten and eleven.

"This next stuff happens fast," she continued. "Stomp your back foot to make the board pop up, just like an ollie. At the same time, drag your front foot forward and off the side. Flick your toe just enough to make the board flip toward you. After the board flips all the way around, it falls to the ground and you land on it. Like this."

One moment, she was standing on her board. The next, she was high in the air, legs tucked up and her board a blur of motion beneath her. Then the board landed on its wheels and she landed on the board.

"Easy, huh?" she said with a grin. "So, you wanna try?"

Mark figured he'd have as good a chance of doing that move as flapping his arms and flying to the moon. He was about to say as much, but he didn't get the chance.

"Absolutely!" Bizz grabbed her board. "I'm going to practice on the grass first. It won't hurt so much when I fall."

"Who said anything about falling?" Savannah picked up her board and carried it to a spot near Bizz. "Me, I plan to crash-land!"

"Do a couple of ollies first, to warm up," Alison advised. The girls nodded.

Now, only Mark stood on the pavement, still undecided.

"C'mon, Mark, you'll never know if you can do it unless you try!" Alison encouraged.

With a sigh, Mark put his board on a patch of grass. He placed his feet as Alison had shown him. But when he lifted his back foot for the stomp that would pop the board into the air, he lost his balance. Arms wheeling, he tumbled to the ground. He lay on the soft grass, staring up into the bright blue October sky. Then a shadowy figure blocked his view.

"Whoa! Excellent fall, man!" It was Xavier Mc-Sweeney, better known as X. X held out a hand, grinning.

"Well, you know what they say," Mark replied. He took X's hand and stood up. "Practice makes perfect."

"You'll have to practice more later, then," X said. "I'm calling a meeting."

CHAPTER TWO

Mark was more than happy to do as X asked. He could feel the beginning of a new bruise from the fall he'd taken.

"Huddle up here, guys," X called. Mark, Savannah, and Bizz joined X and their two other friends, Jonas Malloy and Charlie Abbott, at a picnic table. Alison wandered over to see what was happening.

X reached into his backpack and pulled out a stack of bright orange papers. "It's that time of year again," he said solemnly. He handed a paper to each of them.

Mark read what was on the paper — and tried not to groan. "Uh, oh," Alison said, reading over Mark's shoulder. "I'm outta here." She put her board down and skated away.

ANNUAL TOWN COSTUME PARADE! the flyer in Mark's hands announced in big black letters. CELEBRATE HAL-LOWEEN WITH YOUR FRIENDS!

Halloween was X's favorite holiday. Every year he came up with a crazy costume in the hopes of winning first prize in the town parade. The year before, he'd dressed all in orange and put a real, hollowed-out pumpkin on his head. "I'm a walkin', talkin' jack-o-lantern," he'd said. "See the scary face I carved?"

Unfortunately, X's costume was not a success. Even though the judges agreed it was the most original, they couldn't award X first prize because he hadn't worn the costume for the entire parade.

"The inside of a pumpkin doesn't smell so good," X had admitted later. "Plus, I kept bumping into people. At least I think they were people. Might have hit a telephone pole or two."

Mark smiled at the memory. He couldn't wait to hear what X had dreamed up for his costume this year. Then he looked at the paper again. "Hey, there's a new category of costume this year," he said. "'Groups of three to six people may combine to form one costume.' What does that mean?"

"That," X said, rubbing his hands together, "means that this year, we're all in this together. We're going to come up with the biggest, best, most *outrageous* costume ever! So, any ideas?"

The other kids looked at one another. X sighed. "Okay, I'll think up something. But you guys have to promise me you'll all be in it. Deal?"

Mark wasn't sure he wanted to promise to be part of a costume X had thought up. But he didn't want to disappoint his friend, either. "I'm in," he said. Everyone else agreed, too.

"Great!" said X happily. "Now, what were we doing before I called the meeting?"

"Let's see," Jonas said. "You, me, and Charlie were ridin' the rails. Bizz and Savannah were mastering the kickflip. And I believe Mark was working on his kick-*flop*!"

Mark laughed at Jonas's joke with everyone else. But inside, he was a little embarrassed. It was hard knowing his friends thought he was a klutz.

But what can I do about it? he asked himself. *There's no miracle cure for clumsiness!*

CHAPTER THREE

Mark left the skatepark soon after. He wanted to thank Alison for trying to teach him the kickflip. She'd taken off already, however.

Mark decided to cut through the Square on his way home. The Square was a wide brick street lined with little shops and restaurants. When the weather was good, vendors sold cool stuff from outdoor carts. No cars were allowed in the Square, so it was a great place to hang out. If it wasn't too crowded, kids were allowed to skateboard there, too.

As Mark boarded through the Square, he heard someone call his name. It was Alison.

"I was just thinking about you," she said. She

pulled open the door to a large brick building. "Come here. I want to show you something."

Mark joined her. "Is it okay for us to be in here?" he asked, walking into the building.

"Don't worry," she assured him. "My uncle runs this place." She flicked on some lights.

Mark was standing in a huge room. The floor was wall-to-wall mats. Mirrors covered the front wall. Hanging on another wall were dangerous-looking weapons: long swords, spears, daggers, and short poles joined by chains.

"What is this place?" Mark whispered.

"It's my uncle's kung fu school," Alison told him. "I thought you might be interested in seeing it. Maybe meet my uncle, too."

"Why?"

"Okay, don't get angry at me," Alison said. "But I've noticed that you're, you know, clumsy."

Mark felt his face turn red. Before he could say anything, a deep voice interrupted.

"I was clumsy, too, when I was your age."

Mark spun around. A muscular man came toward them. He smiled kindly at Mark.

"Uncle Eric, this is the kid I told you about," Alison said. "Mark, this is my uncle, Eric Hale."

"Uh, hi, Mr. Hale," Mark said uncertainly. *What did she mean, "the kid I told you about"*?

"Call me Eric. As I was saying, I used to be clumsy, too. When I was twelve, I went through a growth spurt. I went from being five foot two to five foot six in less than a year! My arms and legs felt like they belonged to someone else. Then I found something that helped me." He fixed a steady gaze on Mark. "Alison was thinking it might help you, too."

"What?" Mark asked. *Maybe there was a miracle cure after all!* he thought.

Eric smiled again. "Kung fu," he said.

"Kung fu?" Mark echoed doubtfully. "You mean, like the fighting you see on TV and in the movies and video games?" He turned to Alison. "You want me to learn how to fight? Why? So I can beat up the next person who makes fun of me?"

"No!" Alison looked horrified. "Kung fu isn't all about fighting. It's — it's — oh, Uncle Eric, you explain!"

"Kung fu *does* teach you how to fight, but also to defend yourself," Eric said. "And to do that, you have to practice many different moves. The more you practice the moves, the more you learn to control your body. In time, most people find that they can move with more grace and speed."

"That sounds okay," Mark admitted.

"And that's just one piece of the puzzle," Eric added. "Kung fu is also about learning to believe in yourself. To trust that you'll make the right decisions when faced with problems. Without that piece, kung fu is just another way to punch and kick and block."

"So!" Alison said suddenly. "Wanna learn?"

CHAPTER FOUR

Mark wasn't able to answer Alison's question right away. But he was certainly thinking about it as he left the school. Was it possible that kung fu could really help him become better coordinated? Alison and Eric seemed to think so. But what if he tried it, only to fall flat on his face in front of other students?

"I dunno," he said out loud.

"Dunno what?"

The sound of Jonas's voice jolted Mark from his thoughts.

"I, uh, I dunno if I should get an ice cream on the way home," he stammered. He decided not to tell

Jonas what he'd really been thinking about. Jonas would just make a joke about it.

"Ice cream? Stop by my house," Jonas said. "We've got a freezerful. My dad's working on a new game. He likes to take ice cream breaks when he gets stuck."

Mark and his friends thought Mr. Malloy had the coolest job ever. He worked at home, dreaming up new video games for kids.

"So what's this new game going be?" Mark asked.

Jonas shrugged. "He likes to keep it a surprise until it's done. But last time, I figured it out. He needed to know what the hardest tricks in vert boarding are." Jonas rolled his eyes. "He could've asked me, but no. He got a bunch of lame-o books on skateboarding from the library." He grinned. "Anyway, he left the books lying around. It didn't take a genius to guess what the game was about."

"Books, huh?" Mark looked thoughtful. "Listen, Jonas, I gotta get going. Catch up to you later!"

* * *

Ten minutes later, Mark walked up to the front desk at the public library. Two minutes later he walked out again, empty-handed. The librarian had told him all the library's kung fu books were checked out.

Of course, there was another way to learn about kung fu. When he got home, he hurried to his family's computer and logged onto the Internet. He typed the words "kung fu" into the search bar. A long list of Web sites appeared on the screen.

"Now we're getting somewhere," Mark said to himself. For the next hour, he clicked on different sites. On one, he learned that kung fu is a Chinese martial art that has been practiced for thousands of years. Another site was filled with photos of kids and adults doing kung fu moves. That one also told him that a kung fu training hall is called a *kwoon* and that kung fu instructors are called *sifus*.

The last site opened with a photo of a fantastic-looking creature. It was a Chinese Dragon, a mythical beast with special powers. The site explained that some kung fu schools teach students the traditional

18

Chinese Dragon Dance. When they perform the Dance, the students wear a Dragon costume. The costume has a huge head and a long tail. The dancers in the head make the eyes blink and the mouth open and close. The dancers in the tail make it flutter up and down, like a long wave.

"The Chinese Dragon Dance is an important part of the Chinese culture," the Web site stated. "The Dance has been handed down from generation to generation. Each move in the Dance is carefully worked out so that the Dragon moves with grace."

"Cool," Mark murmured. He wondered if some day he might be part of the Dragon Dance. And as that thought crossed his mind, he suddenly realized he wanted to take kung fu lessons.

Now all he had to do was convince his parents.

CHAPTER FIVE

To Mark's surprise, his parents were very agreeable about his taking kung fu. So three days later, Mark found himself standing in front of the mirrored wall with four other kids, waiting to start his first lesson.

I wonder if they're as nervous as I am, he thought.

"Welcome to the *kwoon*!" Eric Hale walked to the front of the room. "I am your *sifu*, your teacher. Please call me Sifu Hale. Ready for your first lesson?"

Mark and the other children nodded.

"Then do as I do." Sifu Hale clasped his hands in front of him and bowed. As the students imitated him, he explained, "We bow every time we enter the school, before and after each class, and before each fight. Bowing shows respect for your teacher, for each other, and for this school. As you will learn, respect is a big part of kung fu training."

He smiled. "But enough of that. Let's stretch out, then begin the lesson."

Sifu Hale led them through a series of stretching exercises to warm up their muscles. Then he told them to stand in a line facing the mirror. "Today, you'll learn one stance, one punch, and one kick. We'll practice each separately and then put them all together into sets.

"Most kung fu moves have animal names," he continued. "This is the horse-riding stance. See if you can do it." Sifu Hale spread his legs shoulder-width apart, toes pointed out slightly. He bent his knees. Then he made his hands into fists, turned them so his wrists were facing up, and tucked them in at his waist.

The children copied him. When Mark looked in the mirror, he saw he did look like he was riding a horse.

"From this stance, you can move into others. You

can also deliver a punch —" Sifu Hale's right hand suddenly darted out — "or a kick." His left leg flashed up and back. "Let's try punches only to start. Watch yourselves in the mirror."

Mark did his best to imitate Sifu Hale's moves. He thought he'd done them right until Sifu Hale called out, "Mark, move your thumb to the *outside* of your fist. Thumbs *inside* the fist can be broken when the fist strikes something. And when you punch, start with your hand turned up. Then corkscrew it around and strike with your first two knuckles. Those knuckles are the biggest. In a real fight, they'd do the most damage to your enemy."

Mark tried the punch again. Sifu Hale nodded and told him to try it with the left hand. "Both arms and both legs must be able to do these moves," he said. "Otherwise, you're only fighting with half your body."

Left. Right. Left. Right. After ten minutes of punching from the horse-riding stance, Mark's arms were aching. He was relieved when Sifu Hale moved on to kicks.

"This is called a side kick. Bring your knee up to the side of your body as high as you can. Your upper body leans away from the leg for balance. Then lash out with your leg. Strike your opponent with your instep or heel. Try it slowly at first."

Mark was determined do this move right the first time. He didn't want Sifu Hale to correct him in front of everybody again. So with as much force as he could muster, he kicked out to the side with his right leg.

To his horror, the kick was so strong that it lifted him right off his feet! He landed on the mat with a dull thud.

Well, this is just great, Mark thought. He rolled to his back. *So much for the klutz miracle cure.*

CHAPTER SIX

As Mark lay staring at the ceiling, he heard giggles from the other students. He wished the mat would swallow him up. Instead, Sifu Hale pulled him to his feet.

"When you fall, you must get up again," the teacher said quietly. "Otherwise, you will lose the fight. Now, try the kick again, slowly this time. It might help if you separate the kick into four parts. One, knee up. Two, leg out. Three, leg in. Four, foot down."

Still burning with shame, Mark crouched into the horse-riding stance again. He wasn't sure he'd be able to do the kick. But when he broke it into four parts, he found it was easy to do.

He was just getting good at side kicking when Sifu Hale changed the exercise again. "This time, I'll call out different combinations of punches and kicks. Start each combination from the horse-riding stance, and do the best you can. Ready?"

"Yes, *sifu*!"

"Right punch! Right kick!"

Which is my right? Which is my right? Mark thought frantically. He flailed an arm and a leg on the same side of his body, hoping he'd picked the correct ones.

Sifu Hale continued to call out different combinations. First, he paired punches and kicks. But soon he started calling for three moves in a row, then four. By the end, Mark and the others were doing five moves. Mark barely had time to think about what his body was doing before it was time to begin the next set.

Finally, Sifu Hale clapped his hands. "You've all

done a fine job today," he said. He led them through some stretches again, then asked them to sit on the floor. "Each class ends with a short session of meditation. Close your eyes, cross your legs, take deep breaths, and relax."

Mark did as he was told.

"Before our next class, practice what we learned today," Sifu Hale said. "And think about something." He paused before going on. "In class today, some of you thought it was funny when a fellow student made a mistake."

Mark's heart started to pound. *He's talking about when I fell!*

"But let me ask you," Sifu Hale said quietly. "How would you have felt if you were the one being laughed at?"

The *kwoon* was silent except for the sounds of breathing.

"Respect for your fellow students' feelings is very important. Show them respect, and they'll show you

respect. Remember," Sifu Hale added, "you may be the next one to make a mistake."

After class, Mark found it hard to look the other students in the eye. *They probably hate me for getting them in trouble,* he thought. But as he was about to leave, one of the students, a girl named Angie, tugged on his sleeve.

"Mark," she said. "I'm really sorry I laughed."

"That's okay," Mark replied. "I'm used to it. My friends laugh at my clumsiness all the time."

Angie frowned. "Doesn't that bug you?"

"Sometimes," Mark answered truthfully.

"Maybe you should tell them," Angie said.

Mark knew she was right. But he also knew he wouldn't follow her advice. Standing up to his friends just wasn't something he was very good at.

CHAPTER SEVEN

When he got home that afternoon, his mother told him X had called. "He'd like you to call him back. It's about Halloween," she said.

"Oh, shoot!" Mark said. He'd been so busy with kung fu, he'd forgotten all about the Halloween parade. He dialed X's number.

"Hey, bud," X said. "Big meeting at my house tonight to talk about the costume. Jonas thinks he's found the perfect thing. Be here at seven, okay?"

Mark agreed and hung up. He was relieved that Jonas, not X, had come up with the costume idea.

But at 7:05, his relief turned to dismay.

The kids were all seated around the kitchen table,

munching popcorn. With a grand gesture, Jonas laid a book down and flipped it open to a page he'd marked. "Here it is, this year's winner!" he announced.

X pulled the book toward him. From where he was sitting, Mark couldn't see the picture.

"C-o-o-o-l," X said admiringly. "What is it?"

"Says here it's a dragon," Bizz replied, reading over X's shoulder. "Doesn't look like any dragon I've ever seen."

X lifted the book up so the cover was off the table. Mark blinked when he saw the book's title: *The Beginner's Guide to Kung Fu*.

"Hey, where'd you get that?" he asked Jonas.

Jonas rolled his eyes. "My dad checked out every kung fu book the library had. Big mystery what his next game is about!"

But Mark was only half paying attention. He suddenly realized what Bizz had said.

"Let me see that picture," he said, grabbing the book out of X's hands.

"Whoa, steady there, big fella!" X said, pulling the book back. "You'll get your turn!"

Mark had only gotten a glimpse of the picture, but that had been enough. As he feared, the costume Jonas wanted to make was of a Chinese Dragon.

"It's beautiful," Savannah was saying. "I bet I could get some supplies from my mother's shop." Mrs. Smith owned and operated a successful chain of arts-and-crafts stores.

"Excellent, excellent," X said gleefully. "Says here that the frame of the costume is made out of bamboo. Hmm. Where are we gonna find bamboo around here?"

"Maybe we could just use sticks instead," Charlie suggested.

"Too heavy." X drummed his fingers on the table. "I've got it! Cardboard tubes from paper towels, rolls of wrapping paper, and toilet paper! They'd be light enough."

"We're gonna have to use a lot of toilet paper

to get enough tubes," Bizz said. "But I'll do the best I can!"

As his friends continued to joke and laugh about toilet paper, Mark stayed silent. His brain was a jumble of mixed-up feelings. One part of him wanted to tell his friends that dressing up as a Chinese Dragon for Halloween wasn't right. The Dragon is an important symbol of the Chinese culture and to students of kung fu. Using that symbol to win a prize in a holiday parade seemed, well, disrespectful.

But at the same time, Mark didn't want to be the one to squash his friends' excitement. Plus, if he told them what he knew about the Dragon, they'd ask him how he knew about it. He'd have to tell them about his kung fu lessons — and he also wasn't sure he was ready to do that. Not yet.

So instead of saying anything, Mark sat back in his chair and kept his mouth shut.

CHAPTER EIGHT

The next week was miserable for Mark. All his friends wanted to talk about was the costume. They used Savannah's basement as their base, and every day someone brought new supplies. Savannah's mother contributed rolls of brightly colored crepe paper. Bizz found a couple of old sheets to use for the body. Charlie brought tape and magic markers. And on one day, Jonas and X arrived with a box full of cardboard tubes.

"Let's just say my dad wasn't psyched to see a garbage bag full of unrolled toilet paper in the bathroom," Jonas answered when asked where they'd gotten such a huge stash.

Throughout the preparations, Mark's brain was in the midst of a war. One side wanted to tell his friends not to make the Dragon. But the other told him to keep his mouth shut. So far, he listened to the second side. Yet as the day of the parade loomed closer, the knot in his stomach drew tighter.

By Friday afternoon, they had all the supplies they needed. "Be here first thing tomorrow morning," Savannah said. "If we get the costume finished this weekend, we can practice using it all next week."

"Where are we going to practice?" Charlie wanted to know.

Mark's heart pounded. Maybe if they couldn't find a place to practice, they'd dump the idea altogether and his problem would be solved! But his hopes were dashed when X said, "I'll talk to Alison. I bet she could come up with a good idea."

The only bright spots in Mark's whole week were his kung fu lessons. The Wednesday night class started with a recap of what they had learned the first session. He'd practiced the moves at home as Sifu Hale had asked, so his kicks and punches were faster and smoother than before. When Sifu Hale taught them a new punch, kick, and stance, Mark picked them up with no trouble at all.

The next class, Sifu Hale taught them two new moves. The first was an arm block. When done right, the block keeps an opponent's punch from reaching its target. The second was a leg sweep. "The sweep knocks your enemy off his feet," Sifu Hale told them. "It's much harder to win a fight when you're lying on the ground!"

The students practiced the moves alone for a while. Then Sifu Hale had them try the moves out on each other. "One person punches, the other blocks the punch and then sweeps. Since there are five of you, I'll partner up with someone." He chose Mark, and the other four students paired off.

Mark felt nervous facing his teacher. Sifu Hale seemed to pick up on it. "Close your eyes for second, Mark, and take a deep breath," he said quietly. "Trust yourself. You can do this."

And when Mark opened his eyes, he did feel better. He blocked Sifu Hale's punch with a swift upswing of his arm, then swept his leg down low and knocked his teacher off his feet. As Sifu Hale fell to the ground, Mark suddenly and without thinking delivered a punch to the teacher's side.

"Ohmygosh!" he said, horrified at having struck his teacher. "I'm sorry!"

But Sifu Hale was nodding his head. "Don't be," he said, getting to his feet. "You followed your instincts. Those instincts said 'make sure he stays down.' They were right. If it had been a real fight and you hadn't hit me, I might have gotten up and beaten you." He laid a hand on Mark's shoulder. "As I said before, trust yourself. Trust your instincts. They'll usually help you to make the right decision."

During meditation time at the end of class, Mark thought about what Sifu Hale had said. He realized it was high time he trusted himself outside the classroom, too. And he knew what he had to do.

CHAPTER NINE

"Whaddya mean, we can't be a Chinese Dragon for the parade?" Jonas stared at Mark, incredulous. Bizz, Savannah, and Charlie looked equally surprised. The one person who didn't react badly was X — and that was only because he hadn't arrived at Savannah's house yet.

Mark hated making his friends angry. But he didn't back down. "I mean just that," he said. "We can't be a Chinese Dragon for the parade."

Jonas crossed his arms over his chest. "And why not?" he demanded.

Mark tried to explain. "The Chinese Dragon is special to the Chinese culture. To us, it's just a crazy-looking

costume. But to the Chinese, it's part of a tradition that goes back for thousands of years! It feels *wrong* to wear it in a Halloween parade just so we can try to win a prize." He shook his head. "Anyway, I should have said something sooner. I've known all along that what we were planning wasn't quite right."

Just then, X walked into the room.

"Wait'll you hear this —" Jonas started to say when he saw him. But X cut him off.

"I heard most of what Mark said. And you know what? He's right. We shouldn't go as a Chinese Dragon."

He sat down. "I was over at the skatepark, asking Alison where we could practice using the costume. When she found out what we were up to, she kinda said the same things Mark's just said. And she told me something else, too." X stared at Mark. "She told me that you've been taking kung fu lessons!"

Savannah touched Mark's arm and smiled. "You have, Mark?"

He shrugged. "Only a few lessons so far," he said.

"I found out about the Dragon stuff when I was re-searching kung fu."

"Really?" Bizz sounded impressed. "That is just so cool!"

"Man, wait'll my dad hears this!" Jonas said. "I bet he uses you in his new video game!"

As the kids asked Mark why he'd started taking kung fu and what he'd learned so far, relief trickled into his body. They weren't making jokes about it after all.

Of course they're not, a voice inside him said. *They're your friends.*

That trickle turned into a flood when X said, "So, we're gonna scrap the Dragon idea, okay?" Everyone nodded. X picked up a toilet paper tube.

"Now there's just one problem. What kind of cos-tume can we make out of all this stuff?"

Silence fell over the room as the kids looked at the supplies they'd so carefully gathered. Jonas plucked a roll of purple crepe paper from the table. "Maybe we could wrap ourselves up and go as mummies?" he suggested.

"A purple mummy? I don't think so," X said. "Besides, it'll be more fun if we're all part of the same costume."

While they were talking, Savannah taped some strips of crepe paper to a paper-towel tube. She fluttered the tube over her head like a flag.

Or like wings, Mark thought. Suddenly, he sat up. "Guys, I think I've got it!" he said. And as he explained his idea, the others began to smile.

CHAPTER TEN

The day of the Halloween parade was crisp and cool. Contestants gathered at the town hall where the parade was to begin. They would march through blocked-off streets to the Square, where the parade ended.

The youngest group of contestants — toddlers dressed up as cats, clowns, and little witches — started the festivities. Most rode in strollers pushed by their parents.

"No competition there," X remarked as he watched them go.

Next came the kindergarteners and first-graders.

"Half of that group will bail after the first block," X said. "They get tired and start crying for their mothers. I've seen it before."

"'*Seen* it before'?" Bizz whispered to Mark. "*Been* it before is more like it. That's what X did when he was in first grade!" Mark smothered a laugh.

When the second- and third-graders had begun their procession, X called everyone together. "It's almost our turn!" he said, his voice filled with excitement. "Everyone got their inlines strapped on tight? Then get into your positions! Mark, you're in front!"

"What?" Mark almost fell off his skates. "But you're the head! I'm supposed to be behind you!"

X grinned. "Change of plans. We all agreed that since this was your idea, you should be the head."

"You're not afraid that I'll fall and mess everything up?"

"You won't." X thrust the costume's head onto Mark's head. "We trust you."

The head felt heavy, which was no surprise. It was

made of papier-mâché. On the top were two huge bug eyes and long antennae made from wrapping-paper rolls.

Mark tugged the head on tighter. X fastened a sheet they had dyed bright purple and blue around Mark's neck. As he ducked under the sheet, he said, "I'll be behind you the whole way!"

"And we'll be beside you," Savannah said. She gripped one of Mark's hands. Jonas took the other. All three extended their arms out to their sides. Attached to their arms were cardboard tubes. The tubes were decorated with dozens of strips of multicolored crepe paper and aluminum foil. Pipe cleaners held the strips in the shape of wings.

"Look at the bird, Mama!" a little boy standing on the side called out.

Then Charlie and Bizz took X's hands and extended their arms. More wings appeared. Behind them, the tightly rolled sheet formed a skinny tail.

"A bird with four wings?" the boy's mother said.

"No, wait! See the antennae on its head? That's not a bird! It's a — a dragonfly!"

Mark heard X give a muffled *whoop*. "They get it! So far, so good! Now let's get this dragon flying!"

Mark took a deep breath, squeezed Savannah and Jonas's hands, then pushed off. He skated slowly, making sure his friends were following. He needn't have worried. They'd practiced flying so much in the past week, they were like a well-oiled machine. He led them from one side of the parade to the other. From the corner of his eye, he saw the beautiful wings move up and down, slowly and gracefully.

Applause followed them throughout the parade. When they reached the Square at last and took off the costume, X cried gleefully, "Hear that? That's the sound made for a first-prize costume! I can't wait to get on that podium and accept our award!"

Mark hoped X got his wish. But as for himself, he was happy right where he was — flying high with his friends.

Is Kung Fu Right for You?

Kung fu is a Chinese martial art. Buddhist monks were the first people to practice this ancient self-defense technique. Today, people all over the world study kung fu. And it may surprise you to find out that more than fifty percent of the people who learn kung fu are children.

Anyone can study kung fu. But to succeed in the sport, students must be ready to work hard. One session of kung fu can be an hour to two hours long. Sessions begin with stretches to warm up the body. Then students practice different fighting and defense techniques — over and over and over again. This repetition strengthens muscles and teaches students to react quickly and automatically. Quick reactions are important when defending yourself.

Quick minds are also important. If kung fu students don't stay focused on what they're doing, then they will not succeed in a match. So they must learn to discipline, or train, their minds to stay sharp. They are also expected to behave properly in and out of class. Students who throw tantrums, goof off, or cause trouble for others usually don't do well in kung fu.

People who practice kung fu have a lot of self-confidence. They learn to trust themselves. So if having a strong body, a sharp mind, and confidence in yourself sounds good, then kung fu may be right for you!